wHen I woke Up I was A HIPPOPOTAMUS

For my wonderful mum who, when she woke up, was not a hippopotamus. T.M.

For Sabine, Lonneke, Jessie, and Max. R.C.

First published in Great Britain in 2011 by Andersen Press Ltd., 20 Vauxhall Bridge Road, London SW1V 2SA

ISBN 978-0-545-45826-9

12 11 10 9 8 7 6 5 4 3 2   12 13 14 15 16 17/0

Printed in the U.S.A.   08

First Scholastic printing, March 2012

Ross Collins has used concentrated watercolor, vinyl color, and pen on watercolor paper in this book.

WHEN I WOKE UP I WAS A HIPPOPOTAMUS

Tom MacRae

Ross Collins

SCHOLASTIC INC.
New York Toronto London Auckland
Sydney Mexico City New Delhi Hong Kong

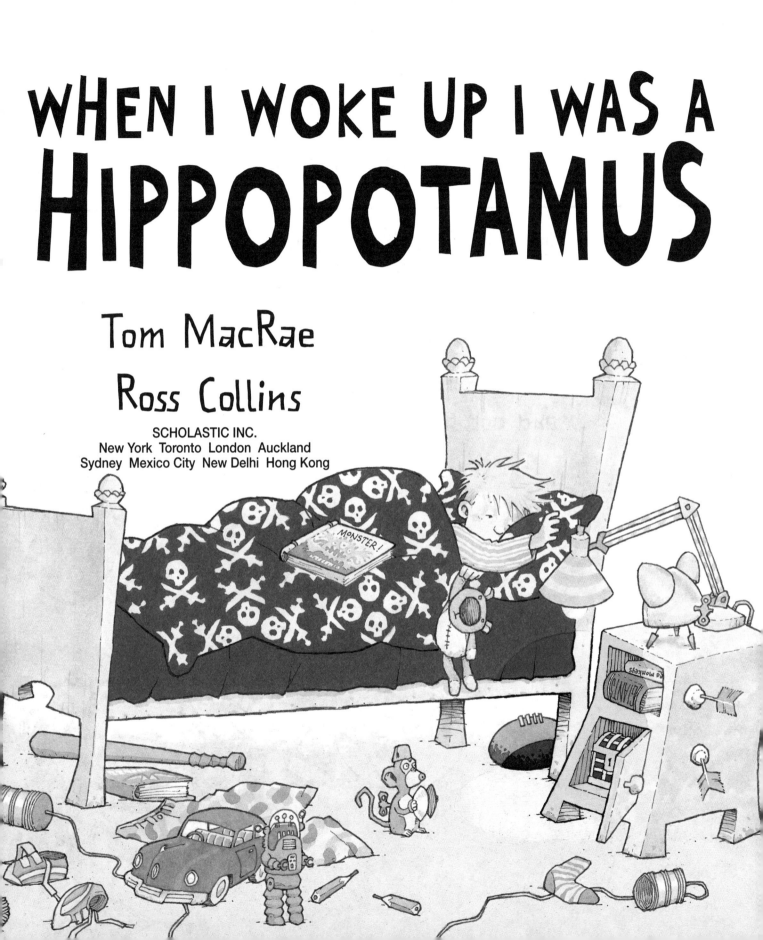

When I woke up, I was a

hippopotamus.

Yawning in the morning, I raised up my sleepy head,
then took one look out of the window
and got straight back into bed.

"Get up!" said Mom. "Or you'll be late!"

But hippos in their sludge
don't get up in the morning,
and so I didn't budge.

My tummy wasn't hungry. I wasn't programmed how to eat.
My mouth was made of metal, like my nose and knees and feet.

"Quick, quick!" said Dad. "Come on! Eat up!
We've really got to scoot!"

But robots can't eat
cornflakes. Dad's words
did not compute.

Malk

Malk

NOW WITH
VITAMIN A

When it was time to go to school, I was a . . .

STATUE.

I couldn't move a muscle.
I couldn't blink an eye.
I couldn't lift a finger.
I couldn't breathe a sigh.

Mom pushed, then pulled.
Dad pulled, then pushed.
They heaved with all their might.

But my legs were made of granite
and my feet were stuck down tight.

When I got to school, I was a . . .
Monkey!

A cheeky little monkey
thought a table was a tree.
I had to climb upon it just to
see what I could see.

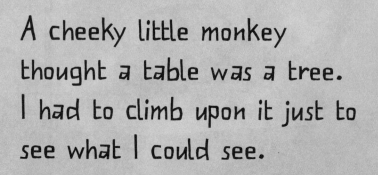

I couldn't sit and listen,
and my work was rather slack.
Then the teacher scolded me—
and made me sit in back!

When it was playtime, I was a . . .

MONSTER!

A scritchy-scratchy monster with ten scritchy-scratchy claws.
I had fifty scritchy-scratchy teeth in scritchy-scratchy jaws.

The girls all screamed! The boys all ran!
My mouth went munchy-crunch!
Then teacher scolded me again
(so I had her for my lunch).

When it was time to go home,
I was a . . .

ROCKET SHIP!

I zoomed up out of orbit,
countdown—5, 4, 3, 2, 1.
I was nearly reaching light speed.
Poor old Dad, he had to run!

My pistons pumped,
my jet packs jumped—
all full of super fuel.
I had to get to Planet Home
and far from Planet School!

When I was in my bedroom I was a... **GIANT!**
My hands were huge as houses, my beard was big and blue.
I was hunting for a human to put in my human stew.
I was crashing 'round my bedroom —well that's just how giants play.
We're big and loud and noisy. We don't know another way.

But Mom and Dad weren't
happy, and they yelled out,

"Keep it down!"

But my giant feet were busy as they crushed a tiny town.
"That's it!" cried Mom and Dad.
"You're louder than **TEN** boys!"
And they stomped upstairs to scold me
for making so much noise.

When Mom and Dad came in, they were ... DRAGONS!

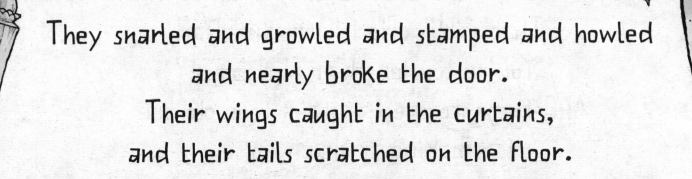

They snarled and growled and stamped and howled
and nearly broke the door.
Their wings caught in the curtains,
and their tails scratched on the floor.

Dad blew a giant smoke ring
with an angry rumbling cough.
Mom wagged a scaly finger—
until I thought it would fall off!

I stared up at my mom and dad
and didn't feel so brave.

I was having fun pretending—
I didn't mean to misbehave.

"Of all the wondrous things," said
Mom, "that you pretend to be,

why can't you be a *nice* thing?"

So I pretended I was . . .

...ME!

We had a lovely evening.
I helped my dad with tea.

Then I read my mom
a story as I sat
upon her knee.

At bath time we played pirates and we plotted pirate schemes.

Then I snuggled in my blanket . . .

...and dreamed **AMAZING DREAMS.**